# Ben's Flying Flowers

Published by
Magination Press
An Educational Publishing Foundation Book
American Psychological Association
750 First Street, NE
Washington, DC  20002

For more information about our books, including a complete catalog, please write to us, call 1-800-374-2721, or visit our website at www.apa.org/pubs/magination.

Printed by Worzalla, Stevens Point, Wisconsin

Library of Congress Cataloging-in-Publication Data

Maier, Inger M.
  Ben's flying flowers / by Inger Maier ; illustrated by Maria Bogade.
       p. cm.
  "American Psychological Association."
  "An Educational Publishing Foundation Book."
  Summary: Emily introduces her younger brother, Ben, to butterflies, which he calls "flying flowers," and when his illness makes him too weak to go see them she draws him pictures, but after his death she no longer wants to draw happy things. Includes note to parents.
  ISBN 978-1-4338-1132-6 (pbk. : alk. paper) – ISBN 978-1-4338-1133-3 (hardcover : alk. paper)  [1. Sick–Fiction. 2. Grief–Fiction. 3. Brothers and sisters–Fiction. 4. Butterflies–Fiction.]  I. Bogade, Maria, ill. II. Title.
  PZ7.M27757Ben 2012
  [E]–dc23
                              2011040290

Manufactured in the United States of America
First printing February 2012

10 9 8 7 6 5 4 3 2 1

# Ben's Flying Flowers

by Inger Maier, PhD

illustrated by Maria Bogade

Magination Press • Washington, DC
American Psychological Association

"Look! Look! A flying flower," shouted Ben excitedly, the first time he saw a butterfly.

"Shhh!" whispered seven-year-old Emily loudly. "You'll chase it away." She grabbed her little brother's hand, and they ran to the clover patch, watching butterflies dance in the air.

"I'm so tired," Ben said suddenly, crouching down with his elbows on his knees and his hands under his chin. There were now **three yellow butterflies** feeding on clover flowers. Emily was sad when she saw Ben was no longer excited.

"Mom! Dad!" Emily called. She was used to seeing Ben this way and knew it was time for him to go home and lie down. She knew this because her parents had explained that Ben was very sick and had a serious illness.

The next days and weeks, Ben and Emily looked for **butterflies** when they played outdoors. Sometimes their parents joined in and they counted all the **yellow, white, and pale blue flying flowers** they found on clover, daisy, and thistle flowers.

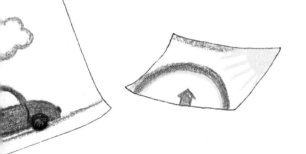

Emily loved to draw butterflies and rainbows.

"Draw one for me," Ben begged when he had to lie down and rest. "Another one! A big yellow one! Now a blue one!" Ben drew pictures too, and proudly taped these on the door of his room.

One day a white butterfly flew into the bedroom.

**"I want you to stay with me forever and ever,"** whispered Ben.

He hesitated, then opened the window and watched it fly to the flowers and then up to the sky.

Winter came, and Ben spent more and more time lying down. Emily drew him page after page of **butterflies** and **flowers** and **stars**. For his fourth birthday Emily made Ben a butterfly pillow.

"My very own flying flower," he said, smiling as he hugged it. The next weeks he took it with him wherever he went.

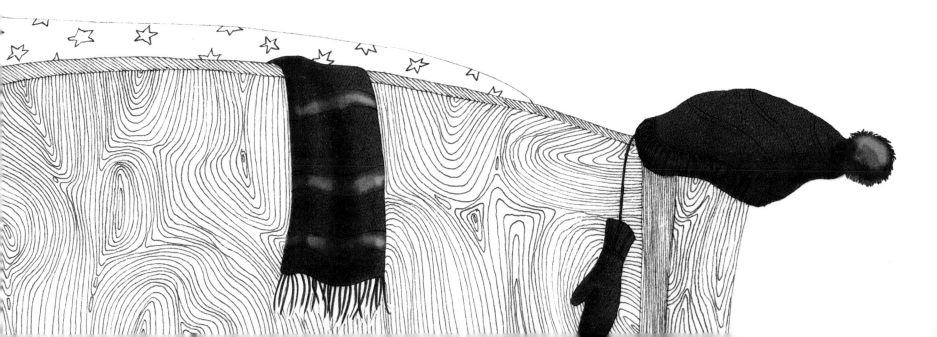

There were more and more trips to the hospital. Sometimes Ben had to stay there for a few days. He slept most of the time, but sometimes he played with his toys and

enjoyed the **doctors** and **nurses**. He didn't seem to be hurting, but after a while he was too weak to lift his arms for hugs. He liked Emily and his parents to sit with him.

One long day, Emily's mom and dad held her close and wiped big tears from her eyes.

"Emily, you know how much we wanted to keep Ben with us forever; how we have all wished. The doctors have tried so hard, but there are some things doctors cannot fix either. Ben was too sick for his body to live any longer. The last word he whispered sounded like flying. Then he looked so peaceful."

Emily's stomach hurt and her heart hurt. Her throat and eyes hurt as she cried and cried with her parents.

"No! He can't be dead,"
she yelled. They tried to comfort her.
"Won't you draw us some butterflies?"
her dad asked her gently.

"No!" shouted Emily running out of the room.
"I'm never drawing
happy pictures again."
Day after day she drew pictures of dark clouds
with rain, and houses with tiny windows and
doors. She missed Ben so much.

One morning, after a rainstorm, Emily and her dad went for a walk. She spotted a **white butterfly** struggling in a puddle. She walked past it, still feeling sad. But then, she turned back, bending down, and carefully lifted it onto a leaf to dry.

She waited and waited until it slowly lifted its wings and flew off.

Emily smiled a big smile. She did not feel angry any more and the sadness no longer felt so big that she couldn't think of

happier things. From that day on she again drew butterflies

and rainbows in bright colors.

The **sad feelings** grew smaller, but sometimes, especially at night, she cried because she missed her brother so much. It

helped when she **snuggled** with her mom and dad.

It helped when she **talked** about her feelings with caring grown-ups. It helped when she did regular things like

go to school, or **play with her friends** and toys.

She and her parents often talked about Ben and remembered clever and funny things he did and said.

"Maybe Ben will come back and live here with us?" Emily said one day.

Emily's mom gave her a big hug. "No, not here like this," she answered quietly. "But we will always love him and think about him."

"What does he look like now?" Emily continued.

Her mom thought for a while before answering. "Close your eyes and think about Ben. What do you see?"

"I see him running after a butterfly."

She smiled as her mom whispered, "Then that can be what Ben will always look like in your thoughts."

"Ben will always be my little brother and I'll never forget him," Emily promised herself.

She held Ben's little butterfly pillow and whispered:

"Flying flowers, flying flowers, white, yellow, or blue. When I see one, I'll remember the special times I had with you."

# Note to Parents
## By Inger Maier, PhD

The death of a child is an extremely tragic and difficult experience for a family. Parents trying to cope with their own grief frequently search for ways to understand and support the other children in the family. The surviving sibling's loss is personal and different than that of the parent. Roles in the family shift, companionship is lost, and self-esteem may suffer as a result. In addition, the child may become an only child. Children can be helped through a sibling's death, though, when the psychological issues are understood and when the child is given support and practical coping strategies.

## Explaining Death to a Child

Families frequently ask how much information to give the child. Some parents think that not saying anything is protective. However, the adults' worried looks and whispered words state that something serious is happening. The child may then interpret this as exclusion from the family and a sign that he is unimportant and less loved. Instead, parents and caregivers should strive to give realistic information in a caring manner and in language the child understands. There is no need for excessive detail, but it is important to check how much your child understands and patiently comfort, reassure, or respond to unhelpful reactions or misunderstandings. Children know the meaning of the word "dead" from an early age, but are not yet aware of its impact. Preschool age children usually believe death is reversible. Given the tendency for magical thinking at this age, some children believe they can wish the person back to life. You may hear, "He's dead now, but can I play with him tomorrow?" A gentle and appropriate reminder that death is permanent can be conveyed with a simple response like "I'm sorry, but tomorrow he won't be able to play either." As children get older, they begin to grasp that death is final. However, they still may not understand their own mortality or realize that young children sometimes die, too.

     Children are helped by understanding that death means the body has stopped working and that the heart has stopped beating. You might say, "When your brother died, his body no longer felt anything, and it can no longer see, hear, talk, eat, or run." Likewise, it is helpful not to refer to the sibling as "passing away," "lost," or "sleeping." Such figurative expressions may be taken literally and could frighten your child or increase bedtime anxiety.

## Common Emotions and Behaviors

Perhaps the first step is to recognize that children do not grieve like adults, but rather express an often confusing range of grief-related reactions. Young children may show their grief with periods of intense crying interspersed with playfulness. Some children withdraw, while others are preoccupied with an upcoming play date. Be careful not to interpret such reactions as uncaring, but understand that this means your child is still unable to grasp or approach the overwhelming loss. Some children may complain of loneliness or boredom or constantly wish to be near the parent. Other children may regress in age-appropriate behavior or become angry and irritable. There may be periods of stomach aches, sleep issues, and nightmares. The child may try to take care of the parent or attempt to show unusually good behavior. She may become anxious about asking questions or expressing emotion, in case it makes the parent too sad. She may also have guilt about past angry behaviors, or jealous thoughts like "My parents would love me more if I was dying."

Fortunately these reactions tend to decrease with time and caring support. If you can tease apart your child's reactions and feelings, you will begin to help your child through the grieving process. First think to yourself: "What does my daughter need right now?" Or "How can I redirect this behavior and acknowledge her underlying feelings?"

## Reinforcing Family Connection and Reassurances

Providing support to your child while you are still grieving yourself is no easy task. However, it is important for parents to support and validate a child's feelings as normal responses. Because children learn so much from you, your child may benefit from seeing you showing sadness and tears after a death instead of disguising your pain by pretending to be cheerful. This not only helps him learn about acts of grieving, but gives him "permission" to express emotion and see that such reactions are normal.

In the days and weeks after a sibling has died, your child will especially need the security and the reassurance of parental love and caring. Try to increase the amount of cuddling and together-time with your child and keep family routines as consistent as you can. Try to read to one another or do an activity together. Having more conversations and phone calls with valued family members is beneficial, too. Also, parents can allow their child to go on play dates and resume activities with friends and classmates. Let your child know it is natural and acceptable to experience some happy periods alongside the sad and anxious times. You may even tell him something like this: "Being happy doesn't mean you have forgotten your sister. It's OK to be happy doing things you like to do."

During the weeks and years that follow, it is very important to remember and to talk about the child who died. You can talk about past hobbies, funny habits, or special characteristics. Talk about enjoyable family times such as vacations, outings, sporting events, or school activities. You can talk about the sibling in every-day conversation, saying things like "Your brother would have loved that movie."

Children will cope better when regularly reminded and reassured of the enjoyment and love they gave to their sick sibling and how this was reciprocated. You can point this out, and help them feel proud of their contributions during the difficult time when their sibling was sick. Similarly, assurance that parents and doctors did their best to help the sick sibling is a helpful reminder and keeps healthy, realistic trust maintained.

## Practical Coping Techniques

Aside from the general guidelines above, there are many practical tools that can be used to help a child recover after a sibling's death.

• Self-Talk. Parents can teach children the concept of coaching themselves through difficult feelings and situations. This "self-talk" is as helpful for children as it is for adults. Give children the words to say, such as "I'm feeling sad now, but I can talk to Mom about this and I'll feel better later."

• **Creative expressions.** Children can be encouraged to express emotions and promote healing through such creative outlets as drawings, puppet shows, or writing letters, stories, or poems. In addition, a child may wish to remember his sibling by creating a memory book that includes photos, art, or lists of his sibling's favorite places, recipes, or books. Memorializing the sibling can give your child an outlet for expressing his feelings, and also helps him carry or display happy memories.

• **New family rituals or routines.** Anniversaries and holidays can be painful reminders of changes in the family, so prepare your child in advance. You might say, "In a few weeks it will be your first Halloween without your sister. Let's think of how we can make that easier. Maybe we could carve a pumpkin for her?" It may be helpful to add new rituals such as a memory picnic or weekend trip. Families often plant a tree in honor of the deceased child or send a parcel to a child in need. Again, check on the readiness of your children before changing family routines.

## Conclusion

Parents may worry that the surviving sibling will be psychologically harmed after experiencing such a family tragedy. However, given positive supports, most children do not have long-term issues, and may in fact show more social awareness and empathy than before. The hope is that with time, the pain will transition to healing thoughts and memories, and that the child will continue to develop and grow as a healthy and happy individual. However, consultation with a mental health counselor is advisable if after three to four weeks the child does not show some signs of relief, and continues to show significant emotional, social, or behavioral distress.